ON APRIL 12, 1861, FORT SUMTER IN SOUTH CAROLINA WAS BOMBED BY CONFEDERATE FORCES, TRIGGERING THE GREATEST WAR EVER FOUGHT ON THE AMERICAN CONTINENT. THE WAR LASTED FOUR YEARS AND KILLED MORE THAN 600,000 AMERICANS. MORE THAN ANYOTHER WAR FOUGHT BY THE NATION. IT ALSO LEFT BEHIND A LEGACY OF HATE THAT TOOK GENERATIONS TO HEAL.

THE UNITED STATES OF AMERICA WAS DISCOVERED BY CHRISTOPHER COLUMBUS IN 1492.

A CONVENIENT SOURCE OF LABOR WAS SLAVES FROM THE CONTINENT OF AFRICA.
Move them to the ship quickly!

THEY WERE OFTEN NOT TREATED WELL.
Come on!!! Work faster or I will whip you.

Education Made Easy

HOWEVER, SINCE INDEPENDENCE, THE COUNTRY HAD BEEN DIVIDED ON THE ISSUE OF SLAVERY.
Slavery is wrong and must be abolished!
But it is a way of life for some people!
I am against slavery.
My workers are free, and paid wages.
THOUGH THE NORTHERN STATES HAD MANY TEXTILE FACTORIES THAT USED COTTON, THEY REFUSED TO USE SLAVES.
THE SOUTH, HOWEVER, DID. SLAVERY WAS VERY MUCH IN PRACTICE THERE.
AS FACTORIES IN THE NORTH PRODUCED MORE CLOTH, DEMAND FOR COTTON FROM THE SOUTH GREW. THIS INCREASED THE LOAD ON SLAVES.
THE PLIGHT OF THESE SLAVES BEGAN TO ANGER MANY PEOPLE, PARTICULARLY IN THE NORTH.
If our Declaration of Independence states that all men are created equal, it is not right for one man to hold another in bondage.
IN1851, HARRIET BEECHER STOWE, WROTE UNCLE TOM'S CABIN HIGHLIGHTING THE CONDITIONS THAT SLAVES WERE FORCED TO LIVE UNDER.
UNCLE TOM'S CABIN
BY HARRIET BEECHER STOWE

THE BOOK WAS A RUNAWAY BESTSELLER.
What a sad life the slaves lead!
Those poor blacks.
Something ought to be done to help them.
IN 1859, A NORTHERN ABOLITIONIST, JOHN BROWN, DECIDED TO FIGHT SLAVERY WITH VIOLENCE.
There's the federal arsenal.
Make for it. We are going to capture it and free all the slaves.
HE AND HIS MEN HID IN THE ARSENAL.
LATER, A GROUP OF U.S. MARINES LED BY COL. ROBERT E. LEE CAME TO CHALLENGE THEM.
BANG!
BANG!

AFTER A SHOOTOUT, BROWN AND HIS ASSOCIATES WERE OVERWHELMED...
...AND TAKEN PRISONERS.
March them out.
BROWN WAS TRIED FOR CONSPIRACY, TREASON AND MURDER. HE WAS HANGED.
THE ACTIVITIES OF PEOPLE SUCH AS JOHN BROWN AGAINST SLAVERY DEEPLY ALARMED THE SOUTHERN STATES.
The Southern States must secede from the Union. We must form a country of our own.
We must form the Confederate States of America.
ONE POLITICIAN, THOUGH MORALLY OPPOSED TO SLAVERY, WAS DEEPLY CONCERNED AND SADDENED BY THE PROSPECT OF SECESSION. HE WAS A LAWYER BY THE NAME OF ABRAHAM LINCOLN.

A house divided against itself cannot stand. I believe the government cannot endure permanently half-slave half-free.
LINCOLN RAN IN THE PRESIDENTIAL ELECTION OF 1860 AS A REPUBLICAN CANDIDATE...
SUPPORT THE REPUBLICAN PARTY
VOTE FOR LINCOLN
GO REPUBLIC
...AND WON.
Hurray for the President elect!
Hurray for Lincoln.
DEEPLY ALARMED AT LINCOLN'S VICTORY, SOUTH CAROLINA SECEDED FROM THE UNION ON DECEMBER 22, 1860...
S. CAROLINA
...FOLLOWED BY GEORGIA, MISSISSIPPI, ALABAMA, FLORIDA, LOUISIANA, AND TEXAS.
S. CAROLINA
TEXAS
LA.
MISS
ALA.
GEORGIA
FLORIDA
THE STATES THAT HAD SECEDED SOON FORMED THE CONFEDERATE STATES OF AMERICA.
Hurray for the stars and bars.
Hurray for the Confederacy!
Long live the Confederate States of America.

JEFFERSON DAVIS BECAME THE PRESIDENT OF THE CONFEDERATE STATES OF AMERICA.
ON MARCH 4, 1861, LINCOLN WAS SWORN IN AS THE PRESIDENT OF THE UNITED STATES IN WASHINGTON DC.
ON APRIL 12, THE CONFEDERATES STARTED THE WAR BY HEAVILY BOMBING FORT SUMTER.
SOON, FOOD AND AMMUNITION RAN LOW.
FINALLY, MAJOR ANDERSON, THE UNION COMMANDER AT FORT SUMTER, CAME TO A DECISION.
We will have to surrender. There is no other way.
AFTER A LONG BOMBARDMENT, FORT SUMTER WAS SURRENDERED TO THE CONFEDERATE ARMY.

WITH ITS FALL, THE CIVIL WAR BECAME A REALITY.
Vs.
THE UNITED STATE ARMY CONSISTED OF 17,000 MEN. LINCOLN CALLED UPON THE GOVERNORS OF THE STATES AND TERRITORIES...
We need 75,000 more men to put down this rebellion.
FARMERS, PRISONERS, IMMIGRANTS, DRUMMERS, AND OTHER COUNTRYMEN FROM EVERY PART OF THE NORTH RESPONDED.
OFFICER ROBERT E. LEE OF VIRGINIA DID NOT BELIEVE IN THE DISSOLUTION OF THE UNION.
The Union must stand.
BUT WHEN VIRGINIA SECEDED FROM THE UNION, HE ACCEPTED COMMAND OF THE CONFEDERATE ARMY.
I cannot raise my hand against my birthplace, my home, my children.
TENNESSEE, ARKANSAS AND NORTH CAROLINA SOON JOINED THE CONFEDERACY.
VIRGINIA
N. CAROLINA
TENN.
ARK.

THE DIE WAS CAST. ELEVEN CONFEDERATE STATES WITH A POPULATION OF 9 MILLION (INCLUDING 3.5 MILLION SLAVES) WERE UP AGAINST THE TWENTY-THREE STATES OF THE UNION WITH A POPULATION OF 21 MILLION.
THE SOUTHERNERS BELIEVED THEY WERE INVINCIBLE ...
RALEIGH TIMES
TUESDAY MORNING, MARCH 1861.
'THE ARMY OF THE SOUTH WILL BE COMPOSED OF THE BEST MATERIAL THAT EVER YET MADE UP AN ARMY; WHILE THAT OF LINCOLN WILL BE GATHERED FROM THE SEWERS OF THE CITIES - THE DEGRADED, BEASTLY OUTSCORING OF ALL THE QUARTERS OF THE WORLD, WHO WILL SERVE FOR PAY AND WILL RUN AWAY AS SOON AS THEY CAN WHEN DANGER THREATENS.'
ON APRIL 25, THE FIRST TROOPS FROM THE NORTH BEGAN TO ARRIVE IN WASHINGTON.
Washington, D.C. Map
THE SOUTHERN TROOPS BEGAN TO ACCUMULATE NEAR ALEXANDRIA AND AT HARPER'S FERRY.
SOON, LINCOLN SENT TROOPS TO OCCUPY ALEXANDRIA, VA. SHORTLY, AT AN ALEXANDRIA HOTEL...
What is this Confederate flag doing here?
Leave it there or I will shoot you!

Freedom for the Confederates!
Long live the Union!
...A FIGHT BROKE OUT.
THE SLAVES OF THE SOUTH RISKED THEIR LIVES TO HELP THE UNION WIN THE WAR.
We would like to help with the war.
ON JULY 18, THE UNION ARMY MARCHED SOUTH TOWARDS VIRGINIA LED BY GENERAL IRVIN McDOWELL.
THE CONFEDERATE ANSWERED WITH AN ARMY OF 35,000 SOLDIERS LED BY GENERAL BEAUREGARD —THE CONQUEROR OF FORT SUMTER — AND READIED TO DEFEND VIRGINIA.

THE MIGHTY ARMIES MET AT BULL RUN CREEK NEAR A RAILROAD CENTER KNOWN AS MANASSAS JUNCTION.
INITIALLY—
The Union has won!
The Confederate soldiers are fleeing!
BUT CONFEDERATE GENERAL THOMAS J. JACKSON HELD FIRM.
Get back on the field!
Long live the Confederacy!
Where are our reserves?
I am going back.
THE UNION ARMY RETREATED.
FOUR THOUSAND FIVE HUNDRED MEN WERE KILLED, WOUNDED OR CAPTURED IN ALL, IN THE BATTLE THE NORTH CALLED BULL RUN AND THE SOUTH REMEMBERED AS MANASSAS.

AS THE CONFEDERATES CELEBRATED THEIR SUCCESS...
Well done, men! They will never invade our sacred Virginian soil again!
...HOPES FOR A QUICK UNION VICTORY WERE CRUSHED.
I need 100,000 more men to serve the Union for three years.
FITTINGLY, THE UNION DECIDED TO BRING IN A HERO OF THE MEXICAN WAR, GEORGE McCLELLAN, TO HEAD ITS FORCES.
HOWEVER, THE WELL-RESPECTED McCLELLAN...
General McClellan has organized the army well.
We can win the war under his command!
...DELAYED TAKING ANY ACTION.
We have been waiting for five months! Why?
FINALLY, IN 1862–
I call for a general movement of all land and naval forces.
AFTER FOUR DAYS, McCLELLAN WAS SPECIFICALLY ASKED TO MOVE AGAINST THE CONFEDERATE ARMY AT MANASSAS JUNCTION.

McCLELLAN, HOWEVER, HAD OTHER PLANS.
We will move south by boat, then march north towards the Confederate capital, Richmond, and take the enemy by surprise.
BUT...
The boat is too big to pass!
We must wait again...
THE CONFEDERACY SOON DISCOVERED THE UNION'S PLAN.
Move the rebels towards the Potomac river to the south.
THIS FAILURE UPSET THE NATION.
Anybody will be better than McClellan to lead the army.
Anybody will do for you, but I must have somebody.
HOWEVER, SOON, GOOD NEWS CAME FROM GENERAL U. S. GRANT IN THE WEST.
We have seized Paducah, Kentucky, and Fort Henry in Tennessee.
GRANT LAID A SEIGE ON FORT DONELSON IN THE BITTER COLD.
I demand an unconditional and immediate surrender.
...AND SIMON BOLIVAR BUCKNER UNCONDITIONALLY SURRENDERED THE FORT TO THE UNION ARMY.

My poor boy! ...It is hard to have him die.
DURING THIS TIME, LINCOLN'S SECOND SON, 11-YEAR-OLD WILLIE, DIED OF AN ILLNESS.
LINCOLN WAS HEARTBROKEN, BUT THE WAR DID NOT GIVE HIM TIME TO MOURN. IN FACT, SOMETHING MASSIVE WAS ABOUT TO HIT HIS FORCES!
THE CONFEDERATE ARMY–WHICH HAD BEGUN THE WAR WITHOUT A NAVY–HAD BUILT ITS FIRST IRONCLAD WARSHIP.
Ironclad *Merrimack* is more powerful than any Union ship!
IT WREAKED HAVOC ON THE UNION FLEET OFF THE COAST OF VIRGINIA.
SOS! The Union's most powerful ship, the *Cumberland*, is grounded! The others are on fire or have run aground!
THAT NIGHT, *MERCURY*, THE UNION'S NEW POWERFUL SHIP MADE WITH A REVOLVING GUN, JOINED THE FIGHT.
We have finally licked the *Merrimack*. Hurray for the Union.
MEANWHILE, McCLELLAN'S ARMY REACHED FORTRESS MONROE BY WATER.

BUT ONCE AGAIN, McCLELLAN WAITED...
All talk and no fight.
LINCOLN WROTE A LETTER TO McCLELLAN SAYING, "YOU MUST ACT NOW". BUT TO NO AVAIL.
MEANHWILE ON THE WESTERN FRONT, CONFEDERATE GENERAL ALBERT SIDNEY JOHNSTON ATTACKED—
THE BATTLE OF SHILOH WAS ONE OF THE BLOODIEST BATTLES OF THE WAR.
BY EVENING, THE UNION SOLDIERS WERE FORCED TO SURRENDER.
Long live the Confederacy!
BUT THE NEXT DAY, 25,000 FRESH UNION TROOPS LED BY GENERAL BUELL ARRIVED.
Fire!
Retreat!
THE UNION EVENTUALLY WON.
Now we have a base to launch an attack on the Deep South.
MEANWHILE, THE UNION NAVY CLEARED THE WAY INTO NEW ORLEANS, LOUISIANA AND CAPTURED THE CITY, GAINING CONTROL OF THE MISSISSIPPI RIVER.

AFTER BUELL'S ATTACK, McCLELLAN FINALLY MOVED TOWARDS RICHMOND, FOLLOWING THE FLEEING CONFEDERATE SOLDIERS.
We will take over the Confederate capital.
BUT ONCE AGAIN, HE DIDN'T STRIKE.
I want 40,000 men under Irvin McDowell for reinforcement before I can proceed.
BUT IRVIN McDOWELL WAS FULLY OCCUPIED AT THE SHENANDOAH VALLEY, FIGHTING THE CONFEDERATE FORCES OF STONEWALL JACKSON.
Stay on guard. Jackson's Confederate Soldiers are trained to ambush and mislead!
JACKSON'S CAMPAIGN HAD SUCCESSFULLY FRIGHTENED THE NORTH.
IN MAY, CONFEDERATE GENERAL JOSEPH E. JOHNSTON WAS INJURED IN A BATTLE WITH McCLELLAN'S ARMY.
We have lost 5,000 men, and the rebels, 6,000, including their commander.
I have heard Confederate commander Robert E. Lee is taking over. He is said to be a good fighter.
LATER, GENERAL LEE ENGINEERED AN ATTACK ON McCLELLAN'S ARMY.
THE BATTLE RAGED FOR SEVEN DAYS.

ALTHOUGH THE UNION WON ALMOST EVERY CONFRONTATION, McCLELLAN'S ARMY CONTINUED TO BACK DOWN.
We must counter-attack!
Lee has lost 20,000 men and is weak.
No! We will retreat.

BY FALL, McCLELLAN'S ARMY HAD RETREATED TO THE POTOMAC RIVER.
We are back and the Confederate capital is still untouched.
Our efforts seem to be in vain.

FINALLY, PRESIDENT LINCOLN SAW NO CHOICE BUT TO REPLACE McCLELLAN...
General Henry Halleck will take command of the troops.

SOON, DURING THE SECOND BATTLE OF BULL RUN, UNION GENERAL JOHN POPE AND HIS MEN MET STONEWALL JACKSON IN A BITTER BATTLE THAT KILLED OVER 25,000 MEN.

CLARA BARTON, KNOWN AS THE "ANGEL OF THE BATTLEFIELD" WAS THERE TO TAKE CARE OF THE WOUNDED AT BULL RUN.

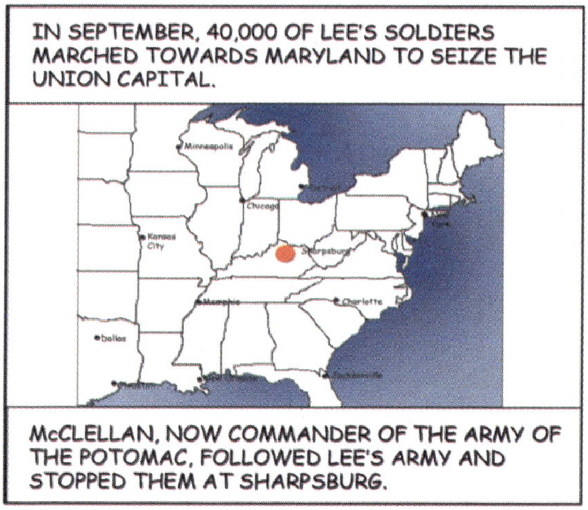
IN SEPTEMBER, 40,000 OF LEE'S SOLDIERS MARCHED TOWARDS MARYLAND TO SEIZE THE UNION CAPITAL.
McCLELLAN, NOW COMMANDER OF THE ARMY OF THE POTOMAC, FOLLOWED LEE'S ARMY AND STOPPED THEM AT SHARPSBURG.

THE INFAMOUS BATTLE OF ANTIETAM BEGAN ON SEPTEMBER 7, 1862.
THE FIRST PART OF THE BATTLE WAS FOUGHT ALONG THE HAGERSTOWN PIKE BETWEEN FEDERAL FORCES AND GENERAL JACKSON'S MEN.
THE SECOND PART WAS FOUGHT BY CONFEDERATE COLONEL JOHN B. GORDON AND FEDERALS ON A LANE THAT CAME TO BE KNOWN AS 'BLOODY LANE.'
BANG! BANG!
THE FINAL PIECE WAS FOUGHT ON A STRONGLY DEFENDED STONE BRIDGE OVER THE ANTIETAM CREEK WHERE UNION GENERAL A. BURNSIDE TRIED TO FIGHT HIS WAY ACROSS.
BANG! BANG!
AT THE END OF THE UNFORTUNATE BATTLE, THE CASUALTIES WERE DEVASTATING...
Drink some water.
...BUT McCLELLAN HAD FINALLY WON A BATTLE, AND LEE'S ARMY HAD BEEN STOPPED.
PRESIDENT LINCOLN WENT TO MEET McCLELLAN.
Lee is weak. Let us finish him off. Go after him.
BUT McCLELLAN FALTERED AGAIN...

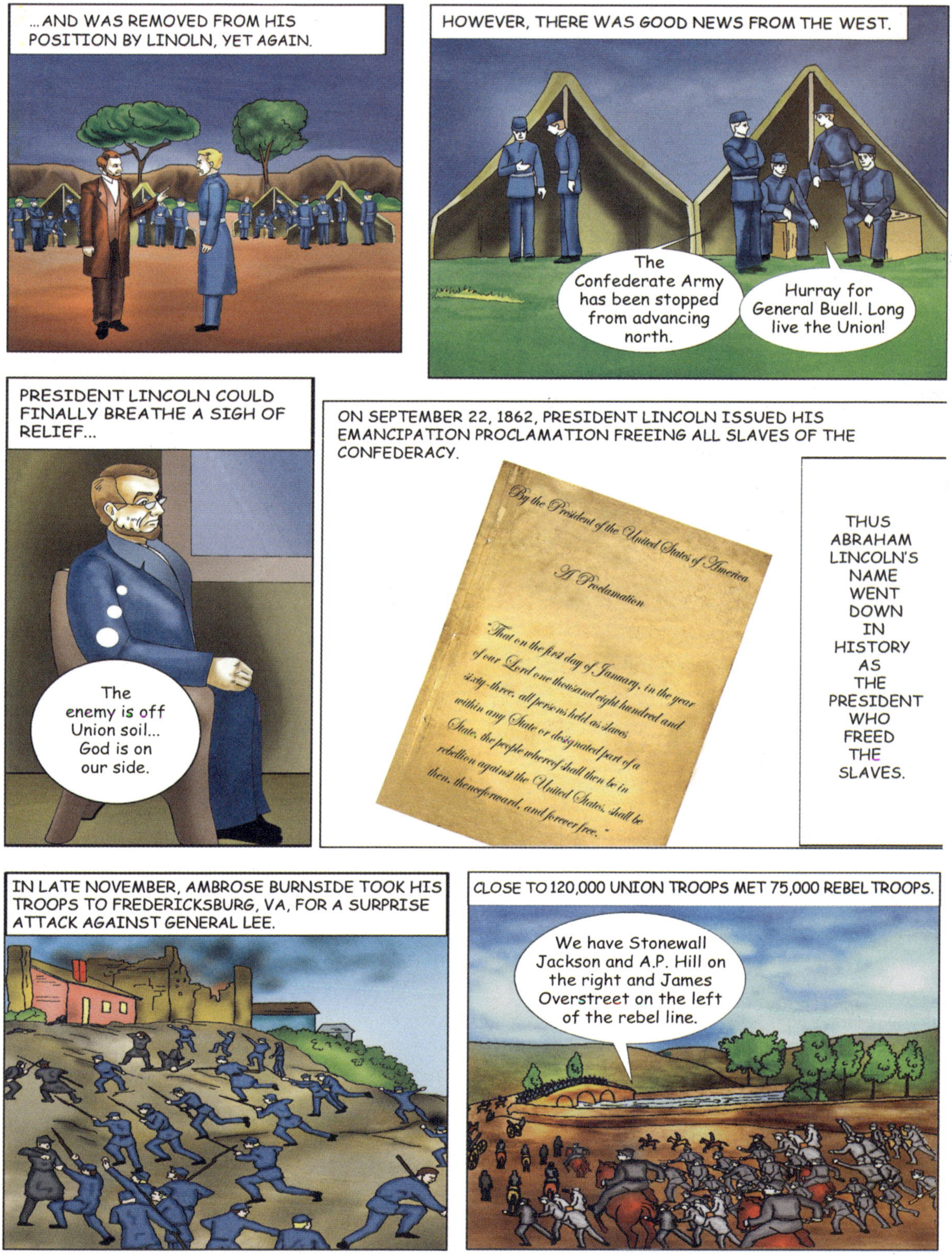
...AND WAS REMOVED FROM HIS POSITION BY LINOLN, YET AGAIN.
HOWEVER, THERE WAS GOOD NEWS FROM THE WEST.
The Confederate Army has been stopped from advancing north.
Hurray for General Buell. Long live the Union!
PRESIDENT LINCOLN COULD FINALLY BREATHE A SIGH OF RELIEF...
The enemy is off Union soil... God is on our side.
ON SEPTEMBER 22, 1862, PRESIDENT LINCOLN ISSUED HIS EMANCIPATION PROCLAMATION FREEING ALL SLAVES OF THE CONFEDERACY.
By the President of the United States of America
A Proclamation
"That on the first day of January, in the year of our Lord one thousand eight hundred and sixty-three, all persons held as slaves within any State or designated part of a State, the people whereof shall then be in rebellion against the United States, shall be then, thenceforward, and forever free."
THUS ABRAHAM LINCOLN'S NAME WENT DOWN IN HISTORY AS THE PRESIDENT WHO FREED THE SLAVES.
IN LATE NOVEMBER, AMBROSE BURNSIDE TOOK HIS TROOPS TO FREDERICKSBURG, VA, FOR A SURPRISE ATTACK AGAINST GENERAL LEE.
CLOSE TO 120,000 UNION TROOPS MET 75,000 REBEL TROOPS.
We have Stonewall Jackson and A.P. Hill on the right and James Overstreet on the left of the rebel line.

We need to attack Marye's Heights.
To go there would be suicide, not warfare.
NINE THOUSAND UNION MEN FELL UNDER THE CONFEDERATE GUNS ON MARYE'S HEIGHTS.
Long live the Union!
BANG !
BANG ! !
BANG ! ! !
BANG ! !
BANG ! !
CONDITIONS AT THE UNION CAMP WERE ATROCIOUS–
Our camps are filthy.
I want to go home.
THINGS WERE JUST AS BAD IN THE CONFEDERATE CAMP–
Everything is getting very expensive. My wife does not have any food to feed our family.
We have nothing to eat!

IN MARCH, 1863, GENERAL AMBROSE BURNSIDE PLANNED AN ATTACK ON THE CONFEDERATES. BUT—
We cannot go in this weather and mud!
Our horses and wagons are sinking.
THE MARCH WAS STOPPED THREE DAYS LATER, AND WAS HENCE KNOWN AS THE ILL-FATED "MUD MARCH".
LINCOLN REPLACED BURNSIDE WITH JOSEPH HOOKER.
I fought with General Hooker in the Battle of Antietam.
He is very courageous.
GENERAL HOOKER HAD A PLAN THAT SEEMED IMPRESSIVE, TO DEFEAT LEE.
THE UNION ARMY WAS TO BE SPLIT INTO TWO PARTS: ONE WOULD STAY AT THE PRESENT POSITION; THE OTHER WOULD MOVE TO ATTACK RICHMOND FROM BEHIND.
ON APRIL 27, GENERAL HOOKER BROUGHT THE ARMY TO CHANCELLORSVILLE, AN ESTATE SURROUNDED BY THE WOODS, AND OCCUPIED THE ESTATE'S LONE HOUSE.
FOUR DAYS LATER, ON MAY 1, LEE'S TROOPS RETALIATED. THEY TOO HAD A PLAN—
Lets us divide our troops. I will take 26,000 Confederate troops and attack the Union on the right side.
Jackson, go and may you win.
We are being surrounded by Confederate soldiers.
They are coming from all around Look out!
BANG !!
BANG !!
BANG !!

AS DARKNESS APPROACHED...
O my God! You shot General Jackson!
What have I done? It is so dark... I thought it was a Union soldier...
ON MAY 10–
We won the battle, but lost our courageous General.
JEFFERSON DAVIS DECLARED A DAY OF NATIONAL MOURNING.
All men will mourn, for truly a great man has fallen.
MEANWHILE ON THE WESTERN FRONT, A NEW GENERAL, ULYSSES GRANT, WAS BEGINNING TO ACHIEVE GREAT SUCCESS.
We have to take the town of Vicksburg, Sherman. I will cross the Mississippi river to get there and seize it.
General Grant, crossing the river will cut off your supplies and reinforcements. Are you sure?
Yes. While you feign an attack on the Confederate Army and keep them busy, I will capture Vicksburg.
CONFEDERATE PRESIDENT JEFFERSON CALLED FOR LEE.
We need to do something about Grant. Send James Longstreet to relieve Vicksburg.
Or, we could attack Philadelphia. That will force Grant to move north to defend Washington.

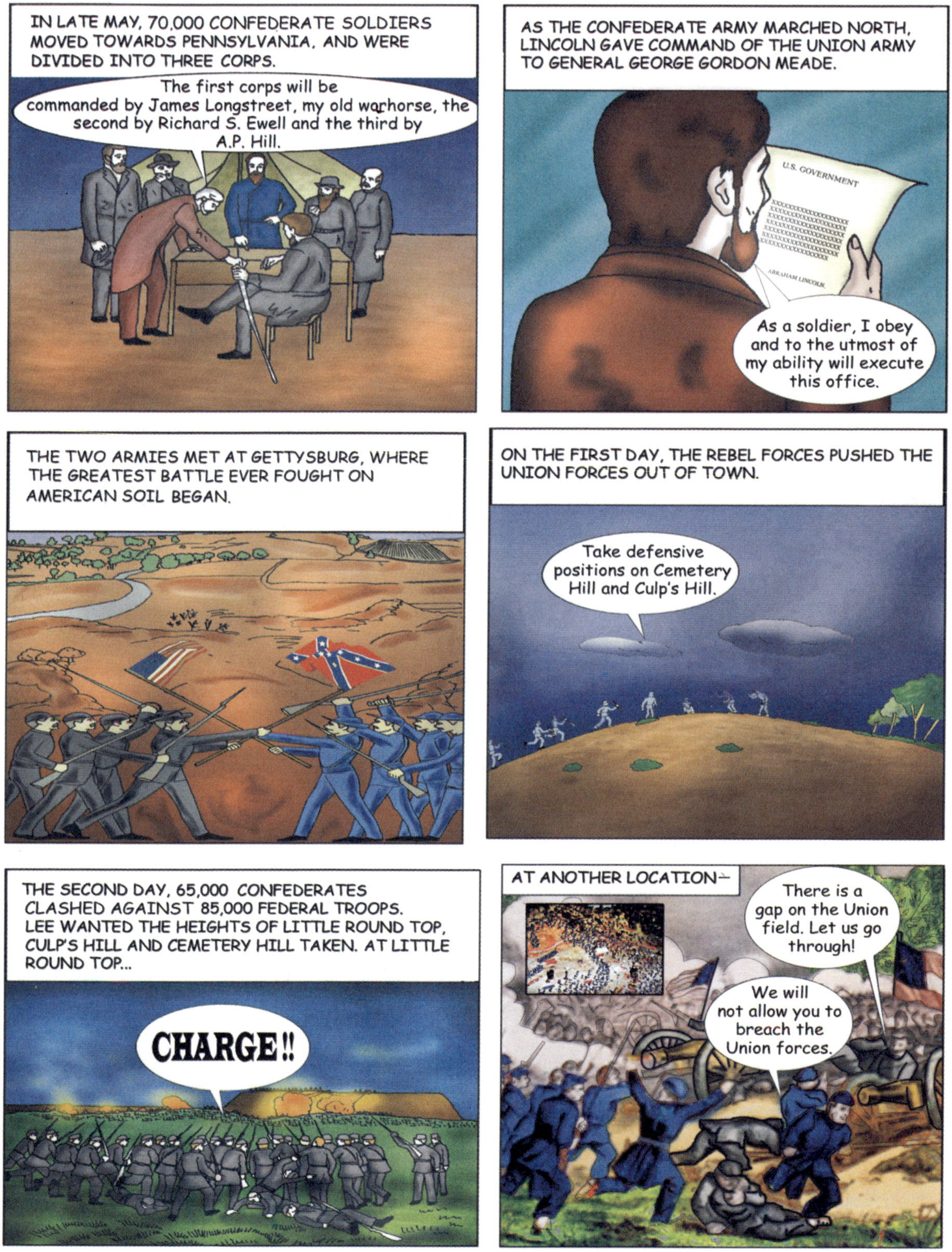
IN LATE MAY, 70,000 CONFEDERATE SOLDIERS MOVED TOWARDS PENNSYLVANIA, AND WERE DIVIDED INTO THREE CORPS.
The first corps will be commanded by James Longstreet, my old warhorse, the second by Richard S. Ewell and the third by A.P. Hill.
AS THE CONFEDERATE ARMY MARCHED NORTH, LINCOLN GAVE COMMAND OF THE UNION ARMY TO GENERAL GEORGE GORDON MEADE.
U.S. GOVERNMENT
ABRAHAM LINCOLN
As a soldier, I obey and to the utmost of my ability will execute this office.
THE TWO ARMIES MET AT GETTYSBURG, WHERE THE GREATEST BATTLE EVER FOUGHT ON AMERICAN SOIL BEGAN.
ON THE FIRST DAY, THE REBEL FORCES PUSHED THE UNION FORCES OUT OF TOWN.
Take defensive positions on Cemetery Hill and Culp's Hill.
THE SECOND DAY, 65,000 CONFEDERATES CLASHED AGAINST 85,000 FEDERAL TROOPS. LEE WANTED THE HEIGHTS OF LITTLE ROUND TOP, CULP'S HILL AND CEMETERY HILL TAKEN. AT LITTLE ROUND TOP...
CHARGE!!
AT ANOTHER LOCATION—
There is a gap on the Union field. Let us go through!
We will not allow you to breach the Union forces.

ON JULY 3, THE REBELS UNDER COMMAND OF GENERAL GEORGE E. PICKETT, ATTACKED THE UNION CENTER ON CEMETERY RIDGE.
THE UNION ANSWERED FIRE BUT SOON FELL SILENT TO LURE THE ENEMY OUT INTO THE OPEN.
AS THE CONFEDERATE ARMY APPROACHED THE GATE—
It is a trick!
God help us!
BANG!
BANG!
BANG!
BANG!
THE BATTLE OF GETTYSBURG WAS THE BLOODIEST BATTLE OF THE CIVIL WAR. FIFTY-ONE THOUSAND MEN, ONE-THIRD OF THE TOTAL ENGAGED, DIED IN IT.
THE NEXT DAY, JULY 4—
Good news! Vicksburg has Fallen. General Grant has taken the city.
The Confederates have finally surrendered after 48 days of siege. The Union now controls the Mississippi.
THE UNION ARMY WAS WINNING, BUT THE WAR WAS FAR FROM OVER. LINCOLN NEEDED MORE TROOPS. BUT—
We will not fight WITH blacks!
We will not fight FOR blacks!

ABRAHAM LINCOLN AND ULYSSES S. GRANT, THE NEW COMMANDER OF THE UNION ARMY, HAD BEEN ENCOURAGING BLACK ENLISTMENT.
By adding the black man, we are adding a powerful ally.
You say you will not fight to free Negroes. Some of them seem willing to fight for you.
ON NOV 19, 1863, ABRAHAM LINCOLN CAME TO GETTYSBURG TO DEDICATE THE NEW UNION CEMETERY AND GIVE A MEMORABLE SPEECH.
Four score and seven years ago...
ON NOV 24, THE UNION ARMY OF CUMBERLAND, COMMANDED BY GEORGE HENRY THOMAS, ATTACKED THE CONFEDERATE ARMY AT CHATTANOOGA.
BANG!
BANG!
BANG!
BANG!
BANG!
THE UNION WON THE BATTLE, AVENGING THEIR EARLIER DEFEAT AT CHICKAMAUGA.
Chickamauga!
Chickamauga!
ON MARCH 8, ULYSSES S. GRANT, WAS PROMOTED TO LIEUTENANT GENERAL.
Congratulations to our greatest general, Lieutenant General Ulysses Grant.

ALTHOUGH GRANT AND LEE HAD NEVER FOUGHT AGAINST EACH OTHER, THERE WERE INTENSE PREPARATIONS ON BOTH SIDES.
IN THE UNION CAMP...
We must attack the Confederate Army from all four sides.
Along with General George Gordon, General Meade will try to capture the Confederate capital.

PREPARATIONS WERE SIMILARLY INTENSE IN THE CONFEDERATE CAMP...
Our goal is to destroy the Union resolve to wage war
We will force Grant to attack fortified positions which will be difficult, and expensive, for the North.

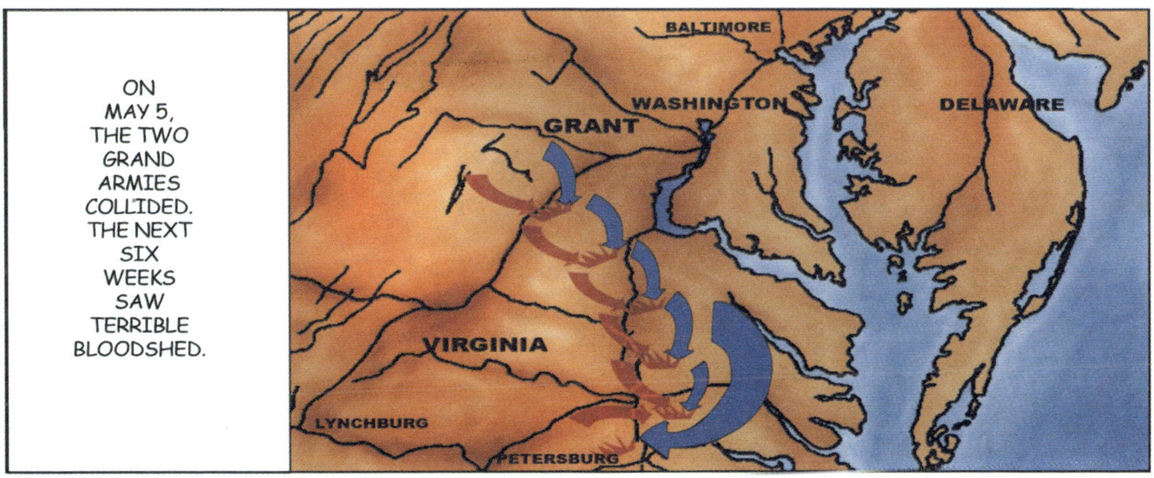

ON MAY 5, THE TWO GRAND ARMIES COLLIDED. THE NEXT SIX WEEKS SAW TERRIBLE BLOODSHED.
BALTIMORE
WASHINGTON
DELAWARE
GRANT
VIRGINIA
LYNCHBURG
PETERSBURG

SOON, AT THE UNION CAMP—
We have lost 50,000 men.
But the general keeps going on.
I have never seen so many wounded and dying on the battlefield.
Once wounded, the soldiers are as good as dead. There is very little sanitization and care.

ONCE THE WARRING ARMIES REACHED PETERSBURG, THEY WAITED 10 MONTHS, AMID CONSTANT CANNON FIRE, TO LAY SIEGE TO THE CITY.
Do you think we will survive?
I don't know. With cannon shells being shot at us everyday, my guess is as good as yours.

AT GRANT'S CAMP...
General Sherman's army seems to be moving towords Georgia.
Sherman believes the people of the South are tired and the war will soon be over.

ON JULY 2, THE UNION ARMY LED BY SHERMAN MET THE CONFEDERATE ARMY OF 60,000, COMMANDED BY JOHN BELL HOOD.
THE UNION ARMY LAID SIEGE TO ATLANTA.
A MONTH LATER—
Hurray! the Confederates have left the city!
ON SEPTEMBER 19, THE UNION ARMY CLASHED WITH CONFEDERATES WHO WERE HARASSING THE SUBURBS OF THE WASHINGTON AREA.
General Sheridan is here. Now we will definitely win!
ON NOV 8, ABRAHAM LINCOLN WAS RE-ELECTED PRESIDENT.
Abraham Lincoln has won the election again.
The people have spoken... We want to achieve the goal we set out to achieve. We want to save the Union!
ON DECEMBER 22, LINCOLN RECEIVED A TELEGRAM FROM GENERAL SHERMAN.
I beg to present you, as a Christmas gift, the city of Savannah, with 150 heavy guns and plenty of ammunition; also about 25,000 bales of cotton.
SHERMAN HAD TRAVELED FROM ATLANTA TO THE COASTAL TOWN OF SAVANNAH AND CAPTURED IT. HIS MEN HAD PLUNDERED AND LOOTED ALL IN THEIR PATH.
IN THE WINTER, SHERMAN MARCHED HIS TROOPS TOWARDS SOUTH CAROLINA.
Here is where the treason began, and , by God, here is where it shall end!
ON FEB 17, 1865, THE UNION TOOK CONTROL OF COLUMBIA, CAPITAL OF SOUTH CAROLINA.

AT PETERSBURG, GRANT'S ARMY STAYED IN A DEADLOCK WITH THE CONFEDERATES, BUT FOR A FEW BREAK THROUGHS.
We ambushed Lee's soldiers trying to escape towards North Carolina.
This war is going to be over soon.
I hope so.
AS SOON AS GRANT RECEIVED THIS NEWS, HE ORDERED AN ALL-OUT ATTACK ON THE PETERSBURG LINE.
It almost makes me sorry to have to fight against people with such devotion for their homes and country.
CONFEDERATE GENERAL A. P. HILL WAS SHOT. GENERAL LEE WAS DEVASTATED. HE SENT A TELEGRAM TO JEFFERSON DAVIS.
My lines are broken in three places. Richmond must be evacuated this evening.
THE CONFEDERATE CAPITAL WAS EVACUATED.
The Confederates are leaving.
The train looks like a Government on wheels.
They are destroying everything the Union can use, including our historical buildings!
TREASURY DEPARTMENT
GRANT'S ARMY OF 125,000 FOLLOWED LEE'S ARMY OF 25,000. ON APRIL 7, GRANT SENT A NOTE TO LEE...
...by asking of you the surrender of that portion of the Confederates States Army, known as the Army of Northern Virginia.
LEE REPLIED...
I reciprocate your desire to avoid useless effusion of blood, and therefore, before considering your proposition, ask the terms you will offer on condition of its surrender.

PEACE BEING MY GREAT DESIRE, THERE IS BUT ONE CONDITION I WOULD INSIST UPON, NAMELY: THAT THE MEN AND OFFICERS SURRENDERED SHALL BE DISQUALIFIED FOR TAKING UP ARMS AGAIN, AGAINST THE GOVERNMENT OF THE UNITED STATES.
- GRANT.
THUS, ENDED THE GREAT CIVIL WAR.
AT THE UNION CAMP...
These rebels are our countrymen again.
We do not want to exult at their downfall.
AT THE CONFEDERATE CAMP...
Boys, I have done the best for you. Go home now, and if you make as good citizens as you have soldiers, you will do well.
I shall always be proud of you. Good bye and God bless you all.

ON APRIL 14, 1865, ABRAHAM LINCOLN AND HIS WIFE MARY TODD WENT TO WATCH A SPECIAL PERFORMANCE AT A THEATRE AND RELAX.
THERE, JOHN WILKES BOOTH, THE FAMOUS SOUTHERN ACTOR, SHOT LINCOLN.
Take that you slave-loving president.
THE PRESIDENT'S WOUNDS WERE DECLARED FATAL AND ABRAHAM LINCOLN WAS PRONOUNCED DEAD THE NEXT MORNING.
WILKES BOOTH, WHO HATED LINCOLN FOR ATTACKING THE SOUTH, HAD TAKEN HIS REVENGE.
THE NATION GRIEVED THE DEATH OF ONE OF THE GREATEST PRESIDENTS OF AMERICA.
In sorrowing tears, mankind has lost a friend and we, a President.